Couch Potato Slices

Short Stories, Musings, and Quotations

by Otto Cleveland

First Printing: 2020

ISBN #: 978-1-71603-186-1

Table of Contents

Preface

I am a couch potato, but I think and have slices. These short stories and musings are some of those slices. I hope you enjoy.

Did you notice that I put *short stories* and *musings* in the subtitle?

You know what short story means, but what is musing?

The Muses were Greek goddesses who inspired the creative juices.

Here are the Greek Muses:

Clio discovered history and guitar.

Euterpe discovered several musical instruments.

Thalia was the protector of comedy.

Melpomene, opposite from Thalia, was the protector of Tragedy.

Terpsichore was the protector and inventor of dance. It was said she put ants in dancers' pants.

Erato was the protector of Love and Love Poetry, as well as weddings.

Polymnia was the protector of the divine hymns and mimic arts. She invented geometry and grammar.

Ourania was the protector of the celestial objects and stars. She invented astronomy.

Calliope was the superior Muse. She accompanied kings and princes to impose justice and serenity.

If a writer sits at the typewriter or computer or an artist sits and stares at a blank paper or canvas, it is said they are waiting for their Muse. Which Muse, would depend on what they are doing. I look at it as an excuse to blame someone or something else for inactivity, but that's just me.

So now onto my Short Stories and Musings.

The Hole

The hole just appeared out of nowhere. One day it wasn't there and the next day it was.

The hole appeared in Isaac Corn's corn field. It was just there. Isaac was walking in the corn field and he heard a peculiar noise, not a loud noise, but a peculiar noise then Isaac saw the hole. It looked like it was made with a biscuit cutter. The edge was smooth. The corn grew right up to the edge of the hole and then nothing. Isaac looked at the hole and saw that it was dark inside. He threw some dirt in the hole and listened for the dirt to hit bottom, but it never did. It just disappeared.

Isaac found the hole the day after Jason Corn was born. Jason was Isaac's son.

Isaac told his neighbor Aaron about the hole and it was just a few days before the whole little farm community knew about it. People were curious about the hole and started to come to Isaac Corn's corn field to see the hole. Sam Smyth, the local sheriff, came to see the hole after it was reported that some teenagers fell in the hole and were never seen again. Sam suggested Isaac put a fence around it until it could be investigated to keep people from falling in, so Isaac put a fence around the hole. Two young men from town brought ropes and fastened them to the ground with large stakes and lowered themselves into the hole. The ropes were taut with the weight of the young men, but then the ropes went slack. The young men were never seen or heard from again. Even with the fence people would disappear into the hole, so Isaac built a building to enclose the hole. It looked like a big outhouse. Isaac put signs around the building and even painted KEEP OUT in large letters on the side of the building, yet people would still disappear into the hole.

The hole was a natural phenomenon and a curiosity and became known as The Hole; The Hole in the cornfield; The Hole in Corn's cornfield; Corn Hole; and sometimes The Corn Hole.

Jason was told about the hole as soon as Isaac thought he would understand so when Jason was four and talking, Isaac took him to the hole. Jason didn't ask any questions he just looked and smiled. As time went by the hole remained a curiosity, but the curiosity seekers became fewer and fewer. It became rare that someone would come to see the hole.

The building that Isaac built around the hole had become ramshackle and the signs faded until they were unreadable. Jason was twenty years old.

As was tradition in Isaac Corn's family, the farm would be transferred to Isaac Corn's eldest son on his twenty-first birthday. Jason would turn twenty-one in a few months, so preparation for the ceremony and the formal giving of the land and house to Jason was being planned. Extended family members were being contacted for their commitment to the tradition. Isaac and his family went to his cousin's Passing of the Land ceremony a few weeks earlier and the adults talked about Jason's coming of age. The Passing of the Land ceremony for Jason was an elaborate affair. Uncles, aunts, cousins, friends and neighbors all came to see the passing of the land. Before the ceremony, there was a lot of handshaking, cheek kissing from the ladies, and pats on the back. It was a fun time. The actual ceremony was much more serious and shorter. Isaac hugged and kissed Jason and it was over. The food and drinks were opened and everyone ate and drank their fill and went home. Jason was beside himself, as the day had not brought the happiness that he thought it would. He knew what he had to do, but it could wait until tomorrow and no longer.

After a long day Jason slept until five, shook the sleep out of his head and body, then went downstairs to the kitchen where his mother was starting breakfast. Jason kissed his mother and went out the back door into the cornfield. He found the hole, looked into it and stepped into it. The hole closed.

"I can resist everything except temptation." - Oscar Wilde

Audrey

The old man walked onto the porch and sat down in a rocking chair. He was born in this old house, as was his father and grandfather before him. His great-grandfather built this house and started a family here. This property was originally a small family farm. To the left, there was once a barn. His father and mother made a living off the farm. It was mostly a dairy farm with a few acres of peas and corn. They sent him to college where he got a degree in engineering. He and his wife had moved in with his father and mother and started their own family when they had a son they named Whitney. Whitney was his father and he moved in with his wife Julia when he got a job in the nearby town. He drove 40 miles to work every day. Farming was abandoned on the property when his parents were in their 70s.

A young man came out on the porch and said, "Hi grandpa, I'll sit with you. The ladies drove me out of the kitchen where I was trying to help clean up after supper."

"Sit down and talk to me Robert," said the old man.

"You know grandpa, if I could, I would take you home with me."

"I know Robert. You live in a small apartment and are just getting started. You've only been married a few months. It will take you a while to get settled enough."

"Alice would take you, but she just had a baby a few days ago and the next few months anyway she is going to have to devote to the child."

"That's all right Robert. Your mom and dad are going to take me and your grandma in."

"I know it must be hard for you having lived in this house all of your life."

"I accept it Robert. I know your grandma and I cannot take care of each other like we should and we need family to help. At least were not going to be put into an old folks' home and will be living with your mom and dad."

The young man reached over and touched his grandfather's hand.

The old man started to ramble.

"You know Robert, I was in the Army when hurricane Audrey came through Louisiana."

"I didn't know that, grandpa."

"It was a 1957. I was stationed at Fort Polk, a few miles north of where the hurricane hit. There were two towns that were devastated by the hurricane. As I recall, they were called Cameron and Big Lake. I looked them up on Google and Cameron is longer than their Big Lake is. We were told that the hurricane took 1800 lives, but Google says it was only 400. My memory is not clear. It's been a long time. Early the next morning after Audrey hit, my platoon was called out and we went into a building where we were shown a film about civil unrest. It showed how troops could go through a town. When we went to the hurricane devastated area, we would use the same tactics to find bodies."

The old man rambled on, "We packed full field backs which included our shelter halves and we were told to pack one change of clothes as extra socks. We were put on 2-1/2-ton trucks and made a convoy to Lake Charles Louisiana. As I recall, it was only about an hour or so drive. Altogether there were about five trucks. One truck held a field kitchen."

"When we got to Lake Charles, we set up a bivouac in a large field. While we were setting up our tents, the bigwigs were planning what to do. It took us a while to set up the bivouac. Everything had to be lined up perfectly. You know that pup tents are made up of two shelter halves two men put their haves together to make a full tent?

"It took at least an hour to set up the bivouac. Then we all gathered around for orientation. Our company commander came out and told us of our mission. We were to go through the areas to help people and find bodies and report where they were, so Graves Registration could pick them up. We were told that we were there because the National Guard was devastated by the storm and couldn't get organized enough to help right now. We were also told looters were stealing things from houses and even cutting fingers off of bodies so they could get the rings. We were told that the looters used pillowcases to carry their loot. We would carry live ammunition in our weapons in case we encountered a looter. Some of the looters were armed and we could shoot to kill if we were threatened by looters. We carried radios to stay in contact with headquarters.

“We went into a town called Big Lake, at least I think that was the name of the town. As the men peeled off to two side streets, I was with a sergeant named Tilly. He was a veteran of the Korean War and a very good map reader. I carried a large radio on my back. I think we called it a PRC–10. Tilly carried a walkie-talkie. Tilly and I came to a dirt road that went to the left. Tilly looked at the map and said there was a building down thc road beyond the trees. Tilly called in our position by radio and told them we were going to go down to the buildings. He gave our coordinates of the buildings.

“Then we went down the dirt road to the building. As we approached the building, a man came out holding bolt cutters and a bloody pillowcase. We brought our weapons up and shouted ‘HALT.’ The man dropped the bolt cutter and reached in his pocket and took out a gun. Tilly and I fired our weapons at the man and he went down. We went up and looked at the man. A bullet had hit his neck and almost took his head off. Tilly called headquarters and told him what happened. They sent out a litter jeep with two guys to pick up the body. Tilly talked to the guys and asked them how things were going. They said they had picked up more than 10 bodies, but this was the first looter. They put the looter in the back of the Jeep and left, then Tilly and I went into the house. It was a two-story building and it appeared that the hurricane had washed water into the first floor. We walked into the house and looked around. We found three bodies; a man, a woman, and a little girl. We called in and told headquarters what we had found, then we went upstairs and looked around. There was no evidence of bodies or anything else. There were snakes on the first floor. We were told that our boots would protect us from snakes, but that we shouldn't reach down as the snakes could strike our arms and hands. We went downstairs to find Graves Registration picking up the bodies.

“We then got a call on the radio that told us to come back and have lunch. We went back to the field. A field kitchen was set up and they were serving lunch. We took our biscuits and got in line. While we were sitting around eating, word came that we should pack up and get ready to go back to Fort Polk, so we struck our tents and packed our full field backs. We loaded on trucks and went back to Fort Polk. We were told that the National Guard took over where we left off. National Guard units from Texas and Shreveport were called in. When we got back to Fort Polk, we were told not to talk about our mission to Big Lake and until today, I haven't told anybody.

“Tilly and I agreed that we would always say we didn't know who shot the looter."

The old man stopped talking and then said, "The mosquitoes will be coming out soon. We should go inside."

They went inside. The ladies came out of the kitchen and sat and watched television.

“Niagara Falls the second greatest disappointment of the honeymoon.”
- Oscar Wilde

Allison Grey

Allison was a martial arts and self-defense instructor at the local YWCA gymnasium. Her classes were on Monday, Wednesday, and Friday from 6 PM to 9 PM and consisted of 5 to 7 members initially, but recently expanded to 20 or 30. The increase in members to her classes was due to a serial rapist in the area. Her students were mostly young women under 30, however she had two older women; one in her 50s and the other in her 70s. Some of the young women brought their husbands or significant others with them so there were a number of men too, however small.

Allison's day job was a waitress in the local restaurant. She worked the lunch shift on Tuesdays and Thursdays as she didn't have classes at the YWCA on those days.

When there was a break in classes, talk invariably went to the serial rapist and how the women could protect themselves.

Allison would say, "Fight, resist, do your best to hurt him. Most rapists are cowards and count on little resistance from their victims. What you have learned here so far can help you to resist."

On the fateful day, Allison decided not to shower at the gym but instead walk the few blocks to her apartment to take a quick shower there and go to bed because she was tired. Allison's shower was a semi-obscure, glass enclosure. A hot shower would steam the glass. Allison disrobed and climbed into the shower, turned on the water, adjusted the temperature, and started to wash. She rubbed soap into the washcloth and ran the washcloth over her body. The shower felt wonderful. She rubbed some soap in her hair because she didn't really want to shampoo and the soap would make her hair clean enough for tomorrow's work. Allison thought she saw movement through the glass door. She disregarded it is as a play on lights in the bathroom.

She turned off the water, opened the door, and stepped out of the shower. A man suddenly grabbed her with both hands on her throat. Allison made a double fist and brought her hands down hard between the man's arms. This broke his grip on her throat. She then brought her double fist down on his face. She thought she had broken his nose, but he wasn't fazed and continued to attack her. She slammed her fists to the right side of his head and he went down. She stood over the man. She had knocked him out. She went into the bedroom, picked up the cell phone off the table and dialed 911. A siren sounded in a few minutes. Allison realized she was sitting on the bed nude so she put on a shirt and a skirt.

The police knocked on her door and she opened it. There were two cops, one a female. The female cop stopped to talk to her about what happened. Allison said, "He attacked me as I got out of the shower and I fought back."

Detectives then showed up to look at the scene. One of them asked Allison what happened and she repeated what she told the female cop.

A few minutes later the detectives went into the bathroom where the man lay.

Allison heard a detective say, "He's dead."

Allison was shocked as she didn't think she hit him that hard.

One of the detectives came back out and said, "Can you come down to the station and make a statement?"

Allison said, "It's awfully late and I'm real tired. Couldn't it wait until morning?"

The detective replied, "We like to get your statement while it's still fresh in your mind. We'll make it as fast as we can. The forensic team will be in your apartment for quite a few hours. Can you stay somewhere tonight?"

"I'll call the YWCA to see if they have a bed in the woman's dormitory," said Allison.

Allison called the YWCA on her cell phone and asked about a bed for that night. The reply was affirmative so Allison said, "Okay, I'll go with you."

The detective said, "We'll drop you off at the YWCA when we are finished."

The detectives drove Allison to the station and interviewed her in the interrogation room. She repeated her story over and over again, then asked, "Can I please go to bed, I'm so tired." The detectives agreed and drove her to the YWCA. Allison checked in, then went right to bed and fell asleep.

Allison woke about 8 o'clock and called the restaurant to tell them she wouldn't be there that day. The manager heard about the killing and understood why Allison couldn't be at work.

Allison walked home to find the forensic team and cops had gone. She went inside and fell down onto her bed. She had only been asleep a couple of hours when a knock on her door woke her up. She went to the door and opened it. There were two cops at the door, one was the female cop that was at her apartment last night.

The cops opened with, "Allison Grey we have a warrant for your arrest."

Allison said, "Let me spruce up a bit and I'll be right with you."

The cops waited while she combed her hair, washed her face, and prepared to go with them.

The male cop read Allison her rights, "You have the right to remain silent." Allison had heard it all before when she watched cop shows on TV.

They put her in the back seat of their car. The female cop turned around and told Allison, "This stinks. The prosecutor got an indictment for you for first-degree murder."

Allison was astonished and replied, "First-degree murder?"

"Don't say anything! You should call a lawyer as soon as possible," replied the female cop.

"I don't know any lawyers," said Allison.

"We have a list at the station," volunteered the cop.

When they got to the station Allison said, "Will you call me a lawyer?"

The female cop said she would as she took Allison into the interrogation room. "Wait for your lawyer, don't say anything to anybody."

Allison sat and stared at the wall. A detective came in and said, "Your lawyer will be here in a few minutes," then he left Allison alone with her thoughts.

Allison didn't understand. All she did was defend herself as it was not her intention to kill the man. She didn't understand why she was being charged. Surely, she had a right to defend herself.

A man then came in and declared, "I am a lawyer. My name is William Greene. Please call me Bill." He then sat down beside her.

Allison looked at the man. He appeared to be about 50 with graying hair and deep blue eyes. He had a kind face that Allison took a liking to him right away and thought, "I like this guy." Allison made judgments fast.

Bill started with, "The prosecutor is saying you enticed the man into your apartment so you could kill him."

"That's ridiculous! He attacked me as I got out of my shower and I defended myself!" Allison exclaimed.

"The man you killed is named Donald Stiles who was the son of a prominent businessman. His friends and family say he couldn't have possibly broken into your apartment, as it's just not him. They say you lured him into the apartment and then staged his attack on you so you could defend yourself then report it to get your name in the paper as an advertisement for your classes in self-defense."

"What a crock! I was attacked and defended myself!" Allison almost shouted.

The door to the interrogation room opened and in walked a dark-haired woman of about 30 years old.

"I'm the Prosecutor. We have a bail hearing in a few hours. I'll be asking for a bail of one million dollars."

"One million dollars?" stated Allison.

"Shut up! I'll do the talking." Interrupted Bill.

The same two cops walked in. "We have to put you in the cage until you go to court," the female one said.

The female cop walked Allison to the cage.

"I've seen you a lot lately. What's your name?" asked Allison.

"Betty is my name," the cop replied.

Bill said, "You keep your mouth shut Allison. I'll go to the court to see who the judge will be. I'll see you there."

Allison went into the cage and Betty shut the door behind her. She was all alone as she sat down on the bench that was there and went into a blue funk. Time went by slowly but Betty and her partner eventually came and took Allison to the court house.

Bill was already there sitting at what was the defendants table. He welcomed Allison and took her by the hand and sat her next to his chair. "The judge is James Orr. He is a fair judge. We should be able to get low bail."

The judge appeared and went behind his bench and the bailiff hollered, "All rise!"

The judge waved his hand and said, "This is a bail hearing. Let's hear what you have."

The Prosecutor started, "The Defendant is charged with first-degree murder. We are asking bail be set at one million dollars."

Bill stood up and said, "That is ridiculous. The Defendant will be proven innocent and has no reason to run. We ask for no bail."

The judge said, "Would you guarantee she's here for trial, Bill?"

"I certainly will," replied Bill.

"It is a charge of murder and I almost always have to set bail, but I agree with Bill and will set bail at $1000."

Bill turned to Allison and said, "I'll take care of bail. Come with me."

As they walked out of the courtroom to the bail counter Allison said, "We never discussed your fee."

"We'll talk about that later. Let's get you out of here," Bill replied.

Bill wrote a check for the thousand dollars. The bail clerk accepted it and gave him a receipt.

"Okay, let's go Allison," said Bill. "You get back to your life. I'll let you know as soon as I do on your trial date. I'll talk to you tomorrow." Bill then left, leaving Allison standing on the street corner.

Allison went to the restaurant to talk to the manager and get a quick cup of coffee. She explained to the manager what had happened so far, that she planned to be back to work the next day, and that the trial would start in about three weeks.

Allison continued her martial arts classes at the YWCA.

The trial date came and she spent most of her day in court.

The Prosecution opened with the facts of the case, "We will show that the Defendant Miss Allison Grey purposely enticed and lured Mr. Donald Stiles to her apartment where she killed him. We will show just how she did this and why."

The Defense countered with, "The charges against Ms. Grey are patently ridiculous. We will show that these charges brought were because the victim was the son of a prominent businessman and owner of Stiles lumber and hardware stores. Your Honor, we ask for dismissal of the charges because of lack of evidence."

The judge denied the request and the trial started.

The Prosecution called the lead detective to the stand, "You were the first detective on the scene. Please describe what you saw and did."

The detective replied, "when I and my partner arrived at the scene, patrol officers Nolan and Gabe were already there. Officer Nolan was talking to Allison Grey. My partner and I went into the bathroom where the victim laid on the floor. Officer Gabe went from the bathroom to the bedroom. My partner, Detective Strand, reached down to the body to feel his temperature and pulse. Detective Strand said, 'He's dead.'" The detective paused as if to collect his thoughts.

The Prosecution urged him to continue, "Please continue."

"The coroner came and looked at the body. My partner and I went to the bedroom to talk to Ms. Grey. Ms. Grey said he grabbed her by the throat when she stepped out of the shower."

"How was she dressed when you talked to her?" the Prosecution asked.

The detective continued, "She had on a shirt and a skirt. The shirt was damp evidently from her wet body when she got out of the shower."

"Did she tell you how she got out of the grip of the victim?"

"She said she joined her two hands together in the grip and brought them up between his arms to break his grip. She then brought her hands down onto his face and thought she broke his nose because the nose was bloodied."

"Did she say she killed him?"

"No, sir. She said she had hit him again because he kept on coming after her."

"Did she say how she hit him?"

"Yes, she said her two hands were joined and she hit him on the side of his head."

"Did she say this killed him?"

"No, she didn't know he was dead until we told her."

"Your witness," the Prosecution sat down.

The Defense said, "I have no questions for this witness."

"The Prosecution calls Conrad Huff."

A rather tall, blonde-haired man took the stand.

"Please state your name."

"My name is Conrad Huff. They call me Connie. I am the owner of Connie's Café."

"Do you know Allison Grey?"

"Yes, she is a waitress in my restaurant."

"You had an incident in the restaurant regarding Miss Grey a few weeks ago, didn't you?"

"Yes, we did. A drunken customer was being disorderly. I went into the dining room to tell him to leave."

"How was Miss Grey involved?"

"The drunken customer grabbed her and she reacted."

"Reacted? How did she react?"

"She hit him."

"Did she injure him?"

"Yes, she broke his arm."

"So, Miss Grey is dangerous."

"She can be, so when the customer grabbed her, she reacted."

The Defense had no questions for this witness.

The Prosecution brought in young women who attended Allison's self-defense classes. The Prosecution's questioning was always, "Did Miss Grey ever say what would happen if the serial rapist attacked her?"

The young women would answer, "Yes, she said that if he ever attacked her that he'd be sorry," or "Yes, she said she would defend herself and make them pay."

Then the Defense would say, "Did she threaten anybody?" or "Did she say she would kill them?"

This line of questioning put the young women in a precarious situation as they wanted to be truthful, but they didn't want to hurt Allison. They would say, "She said we should protect ourselves by fighting back."

"The Prosecution calls Jane Goode."

Jane was sworn in and the Prosecution started to question.

"Have you attended Miss Grey's self-defense classes?"

"Yes, I have," replied Jane.

"Did Miss Grey teach you how to defend off an attacker?"

"Yes, she did."

"Would you tell us exactly what she said?"

Bill objected, "Hearsay!"

The judge replied, "I'll allow it."

Jane continued, "She told us we should defend ourselves."

"The specific? How were you to defend yourself?"

"She showed us how to punch and kick an assailant."

"If your assailant had a weapon, did she tell you how to defend yourself?"

"Yes."

"Did you practice these methods of self-defense?"

"Yes, we did."

"Would you elaborate? Give us more details please."

"I've been going to the classes for almost 18 months. Allison showed me how to punch and kick to defend myself."

"Did she ever say that these methods could kill?"

"She said that these methods could be fatal and that we should be aware of this and cautious."

"Did she advocate killing?"

"No."

"Your witness."

Then Bill took over the questioning, "Did you ever see Ms. Grey intimidating a man?"

"No."

"Did you ever see Ms. Grey challenging a man?"

"No."

"Did Ms. Grey ever say that you should kill somebody who attacked you?"

"No, of course not!"

This is the way the questioning of the witnesses went. The Prosecution would try to get witnesses to say that Allison threatened men and the Defense would try to show that Allison didn't.

The Prosecution put the video in evidence. The video showed Allison talking to a news reporter about the serial rapist in her classes for the young women. The reporter asked, "What would you do if you were attacked by the serial rapist?" Allison replied "I would kill them!"

The Defense tried to make her statement as being just a reaction and anger about the serial rapist.

Then the Prosecution brought in a friend of the victim, Donald Stiles.

"Did you ever talk to Mr. Stiles about Miss Grey and her remarks on TV?"

"Yes, I did and he would say that 'who does she think she is? Does she believe she could defend herself against any man? I'd show her that she couldn't do it!'"

"Did Mr. Stiles take her statements as a challenge?"

Bill objected, "Objection! This is asking for a conclusion."

The judge said, "Sustained."

The trial went on for two days. The judge said, "Today is Friday. We'll reconvene on Monday."

That night the serial rapist struck again. The victim this time fought back and subdued the attacker. The victim had attended several of Allison's self-defense classes. The news about the attack and the woman defending herself was all over the news. Allison heard the news and wondered if it would affect her trial.

Allison went to work at the restaurant the next day, which was Saturday.

The restaurant was all a buzz about the attack of the serial rapist. The victim was Jane Goode. She defended herself and subdued the attacker.

Monday the trial resumed. The Prosecution asked for a continuance because of the incident with the serial rapist and Jane Goode.

The judge questioned why this incident made any difference to the Prosecution. The Prosecution said they thought the rapist was Stiles and would have to rethink their Prosecution tactics.

Again, the judge questioned why the Prosecution tactics would change because they now had the serial rapist in hand, but the judge allowed a continuance until that afternoon.

Bill said to Allison, "This will put a whole new light on our defense." Allison didn't understand why, but they left the courtroom and come back that afternoon.

When they all got back to court the judge asked, "Are we ready to proceed?"

Both the Prosecution and Defense replied in the affirmative.

The Prosecution rested.

"The Defense calls Allison Grey." Allison took the stand.

"Please tell us what happened on the night of the incident."

"I was taking a shower. When I stepped out, a man attacked me and grabbed me by the neck," Allison started her story again.

"Did he say anything?" Bill asked.

"No, he just grabbed me by the throat."

"What did you do?"

"I joined my hands. I brought my arms up between his arms to break his grip, then I brought my hands down onto his face."

"Then what happened?"

"I knocked him down and I think I broke his nose because he was bleeding. He got up and came after me again. I hit him on the side of the head with both of my fists."

"I know you told the story many times, but please continue."

"I left him on the floor of the bathroom and went into the bedroom and called 911."

"Did you report the incident?"

"Yes, I told the operator what happened and she said she would send some people out right away."

Allison continued, "I heard some sirens coming and I realized I was sitting on the bed nude, so I put on a shirt and a skirt."

"Please continue."

"The police knocked on the door and I opened it. There were two officers, one male and one female. The male officer went into the bathroom to look at the body. The female officer sat down on the bed next to me and asked me what happened."

"We've heard the rest of the story over and over again from the officers and the detectives who followed. Do we have to do it again? The Defense rests."

The judge said, "Summations?"

The Prosecution started, "Ladies and gentlemen of the jury we have proved that Allison Grey is guilty of murder. We have shown that she deliberately provoked her attacker and when he responded she killed him. She said Mr. Stiles broke into her apartment and attacked her when she came out of the shower. There is no evidence that there was a break-in at her apartment. We are accusing her of inviting him in and manipulating him so she could kill him. She did this to promote her classes on self-defense in the YWCA. She admits she knew she could kill him but says it was not her intention and that all she was doing was defending herself. Should we believe her? I think not. It is up to you to find her guilty of murder."

The Defense offered the following, "Allison Grey is a respected member of the community and should be believed. When she said Mr. Stiles broke into her apartment and attacked her, we should believe her. The Prosecution says there was no evidence of break-in yet lock picking tools were found on his body. Ms. Grey described in great detail what would happen if she wasn't a martial arts expert. She would've shot him and all would've been forgotten, but because she is a trained martial artist it's assumed that she committed murder. There should be no doubt in your mind that Ms. Grey is telling the truth and you must find her not guilty."

The judge said, "Ladies and gentlemen of the jury, it's time for you to deliberate and find the defendant not guilty, guilty of murder, guilty of manslaughter, or guilty of aggravated assault."

The jury was guided out of the courtroom by the bailiff to decide whether Allison Grey was guilty of murder, manslaughter, aggravated assault, or not guilty.

And so dear reader what do you say?

"If all the girls attending it were laid end to end, I wouldn't be at all surprised." - Dorothy Parker on Yale homecoming

The Coffee Shop

They walked into the coffee shop. "I don't understand how anyone could do that, do you?"

"No, I don't," Al replied.

"I just don't see how he could do that," continued Danny. They sat in their usual booth. "It's a mystery."

The waitress came by, "What can I get you?"

"Coffee," both said simultaneously.

"I just don't get it."

Once again Al agreed, "Don't understand it."

The waitress returned with two cups and saucers in one hand and a saucer with individual creamers precariously perched on a glass coffee pot in the other. She put the coffee pot on the table, placed the cups in front of the men, the saucer with the creamers between them, and filled the cups with coffee then said, "Anything else?"

"Hamburger," said Al.

"I'll have my usual," Danny replied.

"Your usual?" questioned Doris the waitress. "What usual? You've been coming here for almost two years and have never ordered the same thing twice, at least not in a row. What would be your usual?"

"Ok, I'll have a grilled cheese," Danny said and gave Doris a dirty look, "Is that Ok?"

Doris grunted, "Humph," and walked toward the kitchen to place the order.

"Your usual? Your usual? What the hell was that?" Al whispered so Doris wouldn't hear.

Danny replied, "I can't have a usual?"

"Sure, you can have a usual but a usual usually means a regular order," said Al as he unconsciously took the top off a plastic creamer and poured it into his coffee and watched as the liquid in the cup turn a light brown.

Danny also removed the paper top from a creamer and poured the cream into his cup.

"You're an enigma," Al remarked.

"Why do you say that?"

"You just put cream in your coffee."

"Why does that make me an enigma?"

"You have never done that before, so you're an enigma."

"You put cream in your coffee, so you're an enigma too. "

"No, I always put cream in my coffee."

“So, I'm an enigma and you 're not?"

"Sure, ask Doris." Al saw Doris walking to the table with the sandwiches.

Doris set the sandwiches down as Danny asked, "Lois, do you think I'm an enigma?"

Doris frowned at Danny, "Lois? Lois? I've been serving you for two years. Your buddy calls me ‘Doris.’ When an order is up, the cook hollers ‘Doris.’" Doris pointed to her name tag, "And I have a name tag that says ‘Doris’ and you call me Lois? Yeah, you're an enigma, humph."

Al said, "See, you're an enigma."

"Ok, I'm an enigma. I don't like grilled cheese very much and I put cream in my coffee."

"So grilled cheese is not going to be your usual?”

"I don't think so. I don't like the way the cheese tastes, all melted and hot."

"That is what a grilled cheese is, hot cheese."

"I don't like it very much, never did."

"So why did you order it?"

"Lois pressured me."

Al interrupted, "Doris. Her name is Doris."

"Whatever. She pressured me. I don't like grilled cheese," replied Danny.

Al took a second bite of his hamburger, "You're something Danny."

Danny sighed, "I'm an enigma, I put cream in my coffee sometimes."

Al shook his head, "Yep, you 're something else."

Doris came by the table, "Can I get you something else?"

Danny looked up at Doris' name tag. Doris caught his look and quickly put her hand over the name tag and grinned. "What's my name?" she laughed and took her hand down.

Danny laughed, "You caught me."

Al giggled, "I think we just need the check."

Doris snickered and tore the check off her pad, "Ok, here you go."

Danny looked in his coffee cup, noticed it had a little more than a swallow in it, picked up the cup and drank the last few drops. "Yech," he said, "It's cold."

Al said, “I guess we should go."

Danny agreed, "Yep, we should get back.

Al and Danny got up from the booth and walked toward the exit, stopping at the register where Doris took their money.

"Bye guys. See you."

They walked out the door.

“I just don 't understand how he could do it."

Al said, "I agree, don't see how one could do such a thing."

“Cogito, ergo sum.” I think, therefore I am. - Descartes

What Is Your Ethnicity

Today we hear "African American", "Mexican American", or "Japanese American." I think it is time we put American first, like "American of African Ancestry" or "AAA", "American of Mexican Ancestry" or "AMA", "American of Japanese Ancestry" or "AJA" and so forth.

When I first came to Hawaii, (I've lived here most of my life) ads in the newspaper had designations like "AJA", "ACA", and "APA". Although these designations are gone in rental ads, they still turn up in other writings and speech. Even though in speech it is usually fully talked out, "American of Japanese Ancestry". Of course, Hawaii makes a big distinction of ethnic origins as it is almost required to ask of someone's ethnic background. We are very proud of our mixtures. Note I said ethnic backgrounds, not race. We in Hawaii distinguish between Chinese, Korean, and Japanese for example. They may all be Asian, but in Hawaii we say "Chinese", "Korean", "Japanese" or the Hawaiian word equivalency if we know it. Other idiosyncrasies of Hawaii ethnic designations are many, but I will not go into that now.

I want to address "African American" or "American of African Ancestry". Africa is a very big continent and to say "American of African Ancestry" just covers too many ethnic groups. Northern Africa includes Egypt for example. Other parts of Africa include the Watusi, the Pygmies, Hottentots, and many other unique ethnic groups. Of course, you can call yourself anything you like, but wouldn't it be fun to find out if your background included Watusi or some other exotic ethnicity? A massive DNA survey could find the roots of many "Americans of African Ancestry".

Let's go into this more deeply. Not all black people in America were slaves, although most were brought in as slaves. Not all slaves were black, although most were. There were bond slaves that were not black.

Not all black people came from Africa, although most did. Pirate Bully Hayes was a slave trafficker in the South Pacific. Although Hayes mostly supplied workers to Australia, New Zealand, and other Pacific

Islands it is assumed that some Pacific Islander slaves and workers were brought to the United States. Fijians, Tahitians, Indonesians, and Samoans were some of the islanders who were kidnapped and sold into slavery. There is historical evidence that some of these people were brought to The United States.

Ok, now let's address "Native American". This is similar to "African American". Native American covers far too many ethnic groups, from the far north Eskimos to the far south Seminole and all in between. What tribe are you from? Could DNA show what tribes "American of Native Ancestry" belong to? Wouldn't it be fun to find out? Of course it is possible that DNA could be inconclusive and maybe divide us further than we are now, but I believe such studies could bring us closer together because we could then say with pride, "I am American of (fill in the blank) Ancestry," instead of an all-inclusive "African" or "Native". I could be wrong.

For the record I am "ADA". My mother was born in Denmark, so if I get my ethnicity from my mother then I am "American of Danish Ancestry".

"If You Don't Read the Newspaper You Are Uninformed, If You Do Read the Newspaper You Are Misinformed." – Unknown

His Name Isn't Bert

He poured the rest of the jar of salsa into the bowl. He carried the bowl to the easy chair thinking, “I'm just going to sit, watch TV, eat chips and salsa, and just relax.”

He put the bowl of salsa next to the bag of chips on the table next to the chair, plopped into the chair, pressed the on button on the remote, dug a chip into the salsa and took a bite.

“Ooh,” that didn't taste like it did the last time. He put his finger in the salsa and tasted. It wasn't spoiled. Oh yeah, the last time he had to add something to the salsa to make it taste better. He almost threw it away last week when he first opened the jar, but instead he fixed it up. He would do the same now.

He carried the bowl back into the kitchen, opened the refrigerator and tried to remember what he had done to the salsa the last time to make it taste better. He grabbed the bottle of Worcestershire sauce and shook some into the bowl of salsa then he stirred the brown liquid into the red sauce. There, he thought, “that will help.”

He brought the salsa back to the chair and once again plopped himself down and prepared to watch TV. Once again, he dipped a chip into the salsa mix and put it in his mouth, “Yech,” it still wasn't right, so he went back to the kitchen and tried again. What had he put in the salsa the last time? He didn't remember. He mixed a little mustard into the mixture and started back to the chair. “Wait.” He decided to taste it before he left the kitchen. He put his finger into the salsa and tasted it. “Not bad, not bad at all.”
He went back to the chair, put the bowl next to the chips, plopped down and looked at the TV. The volume was muted and there was some kind of action on the screen. Was that guy being chased or was he doing the chasing? It didn't matter. He changed the channel. It didn't make any difference what was on. He just wanted to sit, eat his chips and salsa and not be disturbed. He turned the sound on. He looked at the clock. It was after ten o'clock. The next show was due at ten-thirty. He'd wait. He

muted the sound again. This was the life, sitting, watching TV, and eating chips. He started to doze.

And then the phone rang.

The cordless was on the charger. The hell with it. Let the machine answer it. He'd stay put and have another chip. Besides he could hear the machine from here if it was important, he could call back or better yet, whomever it was could call back. He was busy having a chip with salsa and trying to find something to watch on TV.

He heard his voice on the outgoing message and the beep. Then a female voice started to talk. He sat up and took notice.

“Bert,” the voice said, “This is Cara, please call me back.”

He wondered if she spelled her name with a “C” or a “K”. It was funny how his mind worked sometimes.

The voice continued, “I really need to talk to you. Please call me. I'm sorry,” then the machine beeped and hung up the phone.

Had she left a number, he would call her back and let her know he wasn't Bert. In fact, he didn't know a Bert. He decided when he got up, he would check the Caller ID and see who she was, call her back, and tell her he wasn't Bert, but for now, he had to find a TV show to watch.

He found a show that looked decent even though it was well underway. He looked at the clock. It was 10:45 so either the show, if it was a half hour show, had fifteen minutes left then he could start the next show from the start or if it were an hour show, it had fifteen minutes left and he could start watching a new show. None of the actors looked familiar. Maybe he was watching a movie. He could look at the TV section of the paper and see, but the paper was farther away than the phone. If he didn't get up to answer the phone, he damn sure wasn't going to get up to look at the paper. He clicked the remote to the channel directory. Now he would know what he was watching, as if it made any real difference. He didn't know what channel he was trying to watch, so he clicked the return button on the remote back to the channel. It was channel 43 according to the number in the upper right of the screen. He clicked the return button again and watched as the channel menu crawled up the screen. There was almost always good music with the channel menu. He started to doze again.

Then the phone rang again and again, it was Cara or Kara. “Bert, answer the phone! I know you're home. I saw you come into the building today and didn't see you leave. I'll be in the coffee shop on the corner. I'll wait for you, please.”

She elongated the please as some women do, at least he remembered some of the girls in high school doing it a lot.

Then she hung up.

He muted the TV and surfed the channels. There was an old black and white movie and the actors looked familiar. The actor on the screen was William Powell as he watched Myrna Loy come onto the screen. It was an old Thin Man movie. He liked the Thin Man series and decided to watch for a few minutes anyway. Nick was gathering people for the final showdown. He always did this. He wasn't sure who the murderer was, so he got all suspects together and told them what he knew and hopefully one would say something that would crack the case or maybe even confess.

He turned off the mute and halfheartedly listened to the dialog he'd seen it before, but couldn't remember the outcome.

He couldn't help thinking about Kara (he decided that her name was spelled with a K) and Bert. Was Kara a real dog? Did Bert reject Kara because she was ugly, needy, or clingy? Maybe Bert was a real good lover and Kara didn't want to let him get away. Maybe – why the hell did he care?

Back to the movie. Nick had solved the case and slugged the guy who had drawn a gun and tried to get away. The host of the channel came on and said there would soon be another Thin Man movie then proceeded to try to sell some books and DVDs.

He dipped another chip into the salsa and crunched the salsa laden chip with his teeth. “Ah,” this is the life. He would watch the movie, eat his chips with salsa, and just sit.

But his mind went back to Kara and Bert.

Was it possible that Bert and Kara lived in his building? He didn't know everybody in the building. Hell, he didn't know anybody really. Oh, he recognized some of the people who he rode with in the elevator and could even remember the floors that some them got off on and those who rode to higher floors than he. It was a nine-story building and if every floor was like his, (there were four apartments on each floor) that would be thirty-six apartments and maybe as many as seventy people. He couldn't be expected to remember them all; probably hadn't even see all of his neighbors.

Kara said she was going to wait at the corner coffee shop. There are coffee shops on every corner. The closest intersection to his building has two coffee shops on opposite corners. If Kara was talking about one of them, then which one?

What difference did it make? He wasn't going to go to a coffee shop just to tell her she had dialed the wrong number. He wasn't even going to get up and check the caller ID and call her back. To hell with it.

He dipped another chip and went back to the movie. This Thin Man movie had Nick and Nora Charles in a night club. Nick's old cohorts were coming around to introduce themselves to Nora, Nick's new wife. They all had names like “Spider”, “Fingers”, “Bugsy” and other colorful names. They would say, “Hi, Mrs. Charles. Nick sent me up for five years” or “Nick shot me in the shoulder” and Nora would say, “Oh Nicky, you know the nicest people.” There was a lot of smoking and drinking in the old movies. It was part of the charm.

He tried to watch but his mind always went back to Kara and Bert. She hadn't called in some time now. He supposed it was because she was waiting at the coffee shop for Bert. Maybe Bert showed up and they were talking or maybe she was just waiting.

Anyway, back to the movie. The bowl of salsa was almost empty. He scraped his chip around the almost empty bowl then ate the last of the salsa in the bowl. He still had plenty of chips. He didn't need the salsa, did he?

In the movie there was some sort of conflict between a man and a woman. The woman held Nick around his neck and hugged him. Nora said, "Why Nicky, aren't you going to introduce me to your friend?" Nick sheepishly said, "Nora this is Billy. Billy, this is my wife Nora." Billy let go of Nick and said, "You got married, you rat!" then turned to Nora and said, "I'm sorry, Mrs. Charles. I didn't know."

He didn't hear Nora's reply. His mind went back to Kara and Bert. He got up and brought the salsa bowl to the kitchen. He poured some salsa out of the jar and added some Worcestershire sauce and mustard and this time shook a little garlic powder in it. He had forgotten it the last time, but now it was right.

He went back to his chair but this time he picked up the telephone hand set and brought it with him. He looked at the caller ID and it said, "Private Caller". Kara had her ID blocked. He still didn't know anything about Kara or Bert.

Well, back to the movie. He had been gone long enough for a murder to have happened as he heard the shots when he was in the kitchen. He'd seen the movie before so he could fill in the blanks.
It had been a long time since Kara called.
Then the phone rang. He looked at the caller ID and it said, "Private Caller". Was it Kara? Should he answer it? He decided not to and let the machine get it.

The machine picked up. It was Kara. "Bert, where are you? I waited for an hour."

He was right. She didn't call for an hour because she was waiting and hoping that Bert would come to the coffee shop, but he didn't. How could he have? He didn't know she was waiting.

Kara went on, "All I want to do is talk. Please talk to me!"

Then she hung up.

He didn't know if he felt sorry for Kara or Bert. Kara waiting for Bert and Bert not knowing she was waiting. It was sad.

The movie was progressing. Nick was in a dark place with Asta and Nora showed up. Nick scolded her and they went on to a still darker place.

He grew tired of the movie and decided to change to a news channel. He ate the last of the salsa and chips, turned off the TV, and took the salsa bowl and chips bag to the kitchen. He would shower and go to bed as it was after midnight. He hoped Kara wouldn't call again. It was late. He took the handset back to the charging station, unplugged the phone so it wouldn't ring, showered, and went to bed.

He dreamed about Kara and Bert. His mind put a face and body on both of them. In the dream they were trying to find each other. The dream was all in black and white with Nick and Nora Charles trying to help Kara and Bert.

He forced himself awake. It was 3:14AM according to the digital clock on the bedside table. "Damn." He went to the phone and re-plugged it in. Kara wouldn't call this late, would she?

But she did! He answered the phone "Hello?"

"There you are, why haven't you answered the phone before now?" said the voice on the phone.

“I'm not Bert,” he replied.

“I know you are not Bert. I wanted to talk to you.”

“Why? I don't know you.”

“You know me alright. My name is not Kara.”

“Who are you?” he asked.

“I can't tell you.”

“Can't tell me or won't tell me?”

“Either way, I won't say,” she replied.

“I want to see you,” she continued, “I'll come by your apartment.”

This frightened him a little. “You know where I live?” he asked.
“I know all about you,” was her reply.
Now this was frightening. Had she been stalking him? Why?

“Unless you tell me who you are, I don't want you to come to my apartment,” he said.

“Too bad,” and then she hung up.

It was spooky thinking about this strange woman knowing where he lived, wanting to see him and maybe coming over. It could be he was worried about nothing, after all it was just a woman who wanted to meet him. Under different circumstances he'd be flattered and should be now.

Would she come to his apartment? It was awfully late, or early, depending on the point of reference. 3:45AM was a strange time to have a visitor.

Then came a knock on the door, a quiet knock but persistent. He wouldn't answer the door. He looked through the peephole and saw a dark haired, fairly pretty woman. The knocking persisted. He opened the door.

The woman took a revolver from her purse and before he could react placed the barrel on his forehead and pulled the trigger.

Later that same day homicide detectives were looking for clues in the apartment. They listened to the answering machine recordings. "His name must be Bert," and continued, "Who is Kara?"

One Detective looked through some of his personal belongings found an ID card and said, "His name isn't Bert."

"Celibacy is the worst form of self-abuse." - Unknown

Flatulence

Every year after a noisy New Year's celebration, an even nosier debate over fireworks starts.

Noise seems to be what New Year's revelers want, so what is needed is a way to make noise without all the smoke and fire. I have the solution! Flatulence! Everyone has a built-in noise maker that uses flatulence. All that is needed is to release the flatulence with as much noise as possible, at the proper time.

A well-coordinated flatulence release could make enough noise to please almost everybody and there would be little danger of fire. Although the stink could be offensive to some, there would be no smoke and the gas would dissipate rapidly so air pollution would not be a problem.

We could have contests to see who can release their flatulence with the greatest noise. There could be community coordinators that would encourage members of the community to eat the proper foods to create the greatest amount of flatulence. Foods such as legumes and other high fiber foods are high in flatulence creating elements and are healthy too. Maybe the medical community could develop a pill to help us create large amounts of flatulence. It would be for a good cause.

There could be training for those who are not proficient at releasing flatulence with noise and special practice sessions. A flatulent New Year celebration would be sure to attract tourists eager to participate.

If this catches on, Hawaii could become the flatulence capital of the world. Prior to the New Year's celebration, Hawaii could have an open or invitational contest with the prize being a free entry to the New Year Flatulence Tournament.

Wheel of Fortune could give trips to Hawaii to attend the New Year Flatulence Tournament.

We shouldn't forget historic flatulence like the Captain Cook story about how his ship the HMS Endeavour was saved by flatulence. The story goes that the ship was becalmed in the Pacific Ocean for several days when Captain Cook told his crew to eat lentils for a day to build up flatulence. He then had them position themselves behind and facing away from the mainsails then had them release their flatulence into the sails. The wind generated by the flatulence moved the ship a few feet. With the next few days of using the same tactic, the ship moved out of the doldrums and was on its way to Hawaii.

There were drawings recovered from the Endeavour's logs showing the crew on their hands and knees with their bottoms pointing to the sails. Captain Cook was not the only Captain of the Crown to use this technique to overcome lengthy calms.

The possibilities of Flatulence festivities are endless. A King and Queen of Flatulence. How about a Prince and Princess of Flatulence? It could take the embarrassment out of Flatulence. Schools could have yearly contests with the finals held at the stadium. Every contestant would be given a copy of Benjamin Franklin's "Fart Proudly" book.

"There are two kinds of people in the world, those who think there are two kinds of people in the world, and those who don't."- Robert Benchley

Pink

He woke and looked around. The room was well lit and it didn't look familiar. The walls were a light pink and the bedspread was a little darker pink.

The room was almost an exact cube. The walls were square, each as long as they were tall. The head of the bed where he was sitting up now was against the wall. The bed was a single bed, although it seemed to be standard was somehow different than he had ever seen before. The wall to his left was just pink and except what looked like a door toward the end of the wall, it was blank and pink. The wall adjacent to the wall with the door looked like there was a window that was covered with pink blinds and a curtain. The wall to his right was just a pink wall. He tried to grasp what was happening as he stared at and scanned the room. Sitting up in bed wasn't comfortable as it put a strain on his back. He put his legs over the edge of the bed. That helped a little. The strain on his back continued, so he lay down and thought about what was happening and fell asleep.

Asleep and dreamed. He dreamed that he was on an assignment. That was the only thing that stayed with him when he woke up. He didn't remember anything at all, except the pink room and the "assignment" that came from the dream. What did it mean?

For the first time, he looked at what he was wearing. He was in pink pajamas. The cloth was soft and warm. There were pants with a waist band drawstring. The top was a pullover that had a pocket on the left side of his chest. There were no pockets in the pants. On his feet were pink slippers.

He knew he was being watched and listened to so he yelled, "What do you want from me?" There was no answer. He didn't expect an answer. "Ok, I have to go to the bathroom!" The door on the left side of the room opened with a slight sound. He walked to the door, opened it and looked inside. It was a little room with a toilet and a small sink. Both were pink. He dropped his pants and sat on the toilet. Sitting on the toilet was comfortable for his back. “Wait!” he said to himself. What was it about his back? Why did it bother him so much? He sat comfortably and thought about this predicament.

He relieved himself and sat. He couldn't sit here forever so he got up and walked out of the room. The door shut quickly behind him with a loud noise. He heard the lock engage so if he wanted to go again, he would have to ask.

He walked to the window and looked at it. It was not a window at all, just blinds and curtains made to look like a window. Behind the blinds was just another pink wall.

The light in the room started to dim. It looked like the sun going down. Was he being told that it was getting late? Was it suggesting that he go to bed? Hell, he had spent most of the last hours sleeping, so why should go to bed and sleep? The room continued to darken. He went to the bed and sat on the edge then the room went dark, completely dark. He tried to see a point of light anywhere, but there was none so he lay down and slept again.

He woke when the lights came on. He looked around again and this time there was something new, a chest of drawers! The chest had three drawers and above the flat top there was a mirror. It was a vanity. The chest was pink and the mirror was framed with a wooden frame painted pink. He looked in the mirror and saw a creepy old man looking back at him. He knew it was he, but it was still creepy. The image in the mirror had blue eyes and gray hair. He smiled and the image smiled back at him. At least he now knew what he looked like, but it was strange that it didn't look familiar. It was strange that his face was in a sea of pink. There was little to distinguish the face from the room and the clothes he wore. The face was the only thing that wasn't pink and then he realized he was white! He wasn't sure what that meant exactly or why it was important or not.

He lay back down on the bed. He didn't want to sleep but his back was uncomfortable. It didn't really hurt but it was so uncomfortable sitting the way he was, that he had to lay down again. He slept again.

He woke again. The room was dark. The room started to wake up as it started to dawn. He lay awake and watched the room get lighter. As the room lightened, he looked around. There was something new at the foot of the bed. A chair, a pink easy chair; a chair he thought he could sit in comfort. The room got lighter and he could see the chair more clearly. It was pink, of course, and it was plush. He got out of bed and went to the chair for a look. It was pretty standard with a seat cushion and a full back. He sat in it. It was comfortable. His back felt good! Again, he thought about his back and how uncomfortable he was sitting on the edge of the bed. He must have hurt his back in the past. Now he was comfortable but there was nothing to do, nothing to read, but he was comfortable. He fell asleep again.

He woke and smelled something. It was food. How long had he been in this pink room? He had not eaten since he woke up here. He was not hungry. He looked over to the vanity. There was a tray of food on the vanity. He walked over to it and took a better look at the tray of food. The tray was pink, as were the utensils. There was a fork and a table knife. The food looked familiar; a hamburger patty, he seemed to remember that, and some mashed potatoes. Gravy was slopped all over the tray. He ate and it didn't taste bad; wasn't very good, but not bad.

He left the tray on the vanity and went back to the easy chair, the pink easy chair! “Wow,” he thought how did he get into this predicament? What did he do? What did it mean? Why? He was going to stay awake! There was nothing to do, but he would try not to sleep. He sat in the comfortable chair. He tried to stay awake. Maybe he should try not to sleep. And he slept again.

And again, he dreamed. He dreamed he was walking down a street in what appeared to be a big city. He became aware that he knew he was dreaming. He had read somewhere that if you knew you were dreaming while you were dreaming, that it meant something. He didn't remember what it meant, but something. The street he was walking down was a street that had apartment buildings on both sides; gray buildings with stairs going up from the street to a door on a level higher than the street. The stairs were called “stoops” how did he know that? There were trees growing in little plots of ground. The branches cast shadows on the concrete sidewalk. The shadows and light bothered his eyes.

A man appeared as he walked and gave him an umbrella. The umbrella canopy was pink. He tried to throw it away, but couldn't. He closed the canopy and then he could throw it away.

As he walked down the street it started to look familiar. He thought he recognized it. He looked to his left to the door at the top of the stoop. There was a number by the side of the door, “767”. Did he recognize that number? It was the number of a large aircraft. How did he know that? He was dreaming. He knew he was dreaming, so what he knew now he probably wouldn't know when he was awake. He read somewhere that if you knew you were dreaming while you were dreaming, then that was something special. How did he know that? Was it true? Was it something special?

“If I am dreaming, can I wake up?” He was a little afraid to try. He struggled with himself then he woke up. The room was dark, so he hollered, “Hey there, I'm awake how about some light in here?”

The room lit up.

He said, “I have to go to the bathroom.” He heard the bathroom door open.

“I'm hungry!” he shouted as he walked to the bathroom. He knew that food would not appear if he could see it coming, so he went into the bathroom and sat on the toilet. The door closed and locked. He felt like a prisoner, which he was, but didn’t know why.

He heard the door lock click open. He left the bathroom and walked to the vanity. Again, there was a pink tray with food. He looked at himself in the mirror. He knew it was he, but still didn't recognize himself.

He took the tray and sat in the pink easy chair. The food was pretty much as before. There were some green peas on the tray which added color to the meal.

As he ate, he thought about the predicament he was in. The pink room was confinement. He couldn't leave and he didn't know where he was or why.

The only time he wasn't in the pink room was when he slept and dreamed. Was that the solution? Even though he couldn't leave the pink room physically, he could in his dreams and because he knew he was dreaming he could control the dream, or could he?

He didn't want to appear anxious. He knew he was being watched. He sat in the pink easy chair and tried to relax and sleep, but he was too excited about his idea and couldn't sleep as it was hard to relax.

But eventually he relaxed and slept.

He dreamed he was walking the same street he was a few dreams ago. Trees grew out of little circles of soil surrounded by concrete. This time the trees had leaves, green leaves. To his left, there were buildings with stoops and this time there were people sitting on the stoops. He waved at the people and said, “Hi,” and they responded. The street to his right was traveled by cars and bicycles. There were people and movement all around. As he walked, he came to an intersection where there was a street crossing in front of him and there was a street light. The light was red so he stopped and looked across the street to his right. He could see a coffee shop on one corner. He turned and crossed the street when the light was green. He went into the coffee shop and looked around. There were six tables, four of which were occupied by at least one person, one had two people, and one had none. He walked up to the counter and asked for a medium coffee. He went to the empty table, sat down and looked around. The coffee tasted as he remembered it. Funny thing memory. He didn't remember why he remembered coffee and how it tasted.

A young woman came to his table and indicated she wanted to sit in one of the empty chairs. He said, "Please," and she sat down. She had blue eyes and her hair had a reddish tint.

She said "I haven't seen you here before. Most people here are regulars, so we notice a new face."

"You are right, this is my first time here," he replied.

The young woman continued asking questions and he mumbled some answers. He wasn't sure what was happening, but it was nice and he enjoyed it.

It wasn't long before other young people came to his table and talked to him. For the first time in this dream he looked at what he was wearing. He was dressed much like the young people at his table. Wow, it was good to get out of pink. He knew he was dreaming and knew when he woke, he would be back in the pink room, so he decided not to wake up. He would sleep forever, if he could.

Sleep is Death's younger brother. He never woke up.

"Truly loving yourself is the most difficult thing in the world." - Unknown

Conversation with Margaret

"Men and women are different. Men and women are so different!" Margaret almost shouted.

"Margaret," I said, "You're 23 years old and are just finding this out now? I've known men and women are different since I was about three years old. I mean when I found that boys and girls are different, I just assumed that men and women were different also."

Margaret: "Oh, it's not like I didn't know that men and women are different. I just didn't realize how different."

Me: "Having problems with James?" I knew Margaret and James moved in together a few weeks ago.

Margaret: "When we were dating, he was so different."

Me: "Of course, when you're dating you put your best side forward."

Margaret: "You're right. I know I did and now I do things that drive him crazy."

Me: "The first year of marriage or living together is the hardest because you really get to know each other."

Margaret: "He does things like sitting around on the couch drinking beer burping and farting. He didn't do that before."

Me: "You should be flattered he's comfortable enough with you to really be himself."

Margaret: "I know you're right. I just didn't think it would be this hard to adjust. And then there's the toilet seat."

Me: "The toilet seat, are you serious? This is the biggest problem most young couples. Your family dynamics. You were probably raised in a house that catered to girls and he was raised in a house that didn't."

Margaret: "You're right. Why should it be so difficult for him to lower the seat?"

Me: "He was probably trained to raise the seat when he peed. If he didn't, he would get scolded because the females in the family would sit on a wet seat, so he was trained that way."

Margaret: "So I have to retrain?"

Me: "That's right, but is fairly easy to do. You just keep reminding him and when you finish you raise the seat. This way you will always know the seat is up and if he ever has to sit and doesn't raise the seat, he would remember to lower the seat for you the next time."

Margaret: "So I have to train him?"

Me: "It's said that a man will marry a woman hoping she will never change and a woman will marry a man hoping he can change, but both are wrong."

Margaret: "So, he'll never change?"

Me: "I didn't say that. He will change and you will change and it's part of the family dynamic you will put together."

Margaret: "What you mean?"

Me: "I mean the longer you stay together, the more you will adjust to the other person. Both of you will adjust. You will change and he will change."

Margaret: "So I will just have to put up with it until he changes?"

Me: "Both of you will have to put up with each other until both of you change or get used to the fact that you won't change."

Margaret: "How long will it be before he changes?"

Me: "It's a process. Don't expect him to change and you not. You both have to change and get used to being with each other. You have to decide what's important and what's not."

Margaret: "And then there's sex. He wants sex all the time and I don't."

Me: "Trust me he doesn't want sex all the time. He only thinks he wants sex all the time."

Margaret: "So what can I do?"

Me: "Give him sex whenever he wants it. The time will come when he won't be able to perform."

Margaret: "When will that be? I'll be exhausted."

Me: "You'll be exhausted and when he can't perform, you'll have to treat his bruised ego."

Margaret: "What do you mean, treat his ego?"

Me: "A man's ego surrounds his penis. If he can't perform, then his ego is crushed. You have to treat it by controlling, cuddling, and saying sweet words and sharing with him that it's all right."

Margaret: "Are you saying that all couples go through this period of adjustment?"

Me: "Exactly. All are different. Others adjust very easily. It depends on their family dynamic in the way they were raised".

Margaret: "So I just have to hang in there?"

Me: "Don't forget that it's hard for him too. You both have to adjust to each other. You have to make the effort and so does he."

Margaret: "So we just have to wait to see what happens?"

Me: "That's about it."

"I require only three things of a man. He must be handsome, ruthless and stupid." - Dorothy Parker

Phoebe - My Maiden Aunt

Brian Coster and his mother and father moved to the little Florida town right after the Second World War ended. He was a young boy of about eight years old, so he didn't remember a lot about the early years he spent there.

He remembered that most of the streets were not paved but were gray, fine sand. There were two paved streets that crossed, although he didn't remember the names or numbers of the streets. He did remember that streets and avenues ran in opposite directions. Streets went north and south while avenues went east and west, or maybe vice versa. He remembered taking a streetcar to Saint Petersburg on Saturdays and going to the movies. On some Saturdays, there were all cartoon shows and he really liked that.

But mostly he remembered his Aunt Phoebe. Aunt Phoebe would always phone the day before she came and that would start an argument between Brian's mom and dad. Dad would say he didn't like Aunt Phoebe coming to visit and mom would say, "She's my sister. I can't tell her not to come, can I?" The next day Aunt Phoebe would drive up to the house in a flashy car, honk the horn, and Brian's mother would run out the front door shouting, "Phoebe! Phoebe!" then she and Aunt Phoebe would carry a suitcase and a shopping bag into the house. The shopping bag, it turned out, was always gifts for mom, dad, and Brian. Although his mother would always be enthusiastic about Aunt Phoebe's visit, his father was less than happy about it.

Aunt Phoebe would always open the bag of gifts, give mom a kitchen gadget of some kind and give dad a neck tie or a set consisting of a tie and some handkerchiefs or maybe just some socks. Aunt Phoebe would always say, "Jack you are so hard to buy for. I never know what to get for you and Doris doesn't give me a clue."

Then came Brian's gift. Aunt Phoebe would say, "I don't know what a nine-year-old boy wants except maybe a nine-year-old girl," then she would laugh and give Brian a big hug. Brian's gift was always a toy of some kind or a board game. Brian liked the hug more than the gift. Brian liked Aunt Phoebe and as the years went by Aunt Phoebe would pay more and more attention to him.

Mom and Aunt Phoebe would talk, laugh and in general, have a good time for the few days Aunt Phoebe stayed. They would chatter far into the night while dad would almost ignore Aunt Phoebe. Sometimes Aunt Phoebe and mom would go in the back yard and talk softly in whispers.

Aunt Phoebe would visit two or three times a year but never on holidays. Once when Brian was ten years old and it was about time for Aunt Phoebe to call about her upcoming visit, the phone rang and Brian's mom cried into the phone and said, “Oh no, Phoebe, I'm so sorry, my God! Please let us know what happens.” She hung up the phone and simply said, “Phoebe won't be coming for a little while.”

Brian's dad looked pleased while his mom was obviously shaken by the phone call. Brian didn't know what it was all about until late that night when his parents thought he was asleep.

“Jack,” his mom started, “Phoebe's been arrested.”

“I'm not surprised,” his dad said, “the kind of life she leads.”

“We have to help her!”

“Of course, if we can.” Jack said reluctantly.

Brian had heard enough. He didn't want to know anything bad about Aunt Phoebe, so he went to sleep.

The next day Brian had to go to school. His mom packed his lunch and saw him off. When Brian returned from school his dad met him at the door and said, “your mom has gone to visit your Aunt Phoebe so it's just us guys 'till she gets back.”

Brian knew that his mom had gone to help Aunt Phoebe. He tried not to show his dad that he knew Aunt Phoebe was in trouble.

The next day was Saturday. Brian's dad gave him money to go to the movies in Saint Petersburg. He said he had to stay by the phone in case his mom called. Brian reluctantly went to the movies. He knew it would do no good for him to stay by the phone with his dad, but he wanted to know what was happening. When Brian got home from the movies, his dad said, "your mom is coming home tomorrow with Aunt Phoebe."

The next morning Brian's mom drove up in Aunt Phoebe's car. Aunt Phoebe looked tired and was pale and ashen. Aunt Phoebe stumbled up the walk with mom helping her. Aunt Phoebe was sick! Brian was shocked to see Aunt Phoebe looking so badly. Brian's mom took Aunt Phoebe into the room where Aunt Phoebe always stayed when she visited. Mom came out a few minutes later with her index finger on her lips. "She's sleeping. Let's try and be quiet."

Brian whispered, "what happened mom?" She answered, "we can talk later."

It was two days before Aunt Phoebe came out of her room except to go to the bathroom and when she came out it was only to eat breakfast. The next few days Aunt Phoebe spent more and more time outside her room and started to look better and better. It looked like she was really getting better. As Aunt Phoebe was recovering, she and Brian would have long talks on the front porch. Mostly the talks were about Brian and his mom and dad. Did they get along? Did they seem happy? Did they treat Brian well? Sometimes they would just talk like he did with some of his friends at school. Sometimes his friends from school would visit and Aunt Phoebe would talk to them as if she were one of them. She made them comfortable with her and she with them.

One Saturday Aunt Phoebe took Brian to Tampa where they spent the day just being together. They shopped and ate lunch at a nice restaurant. Brian asked, "Where do you live?" Aunt Phoebe answered, "Mostly I live in Orlando, but I sometimes live in Jacksonville and sometimes in Miami," she continued, "It's when I'm going to Orlando from

Jacksonville or Miami that I stop off to see you and your mom." Brian noticed that Aunt Phoebe didn't mention his father.

Then Sunday came and Aunt Phoebe left with promises of returning soon.

The next time Aunt Phoebe came to visit, she brought some large boxes. Jack and Doris helped her bring the boxes in the house and into her room. Brian thought they were expecting Aunt Phoebe to bring the boxes.

Aunt Phoebe said, "The next time I visit I will bring the rest of the things."

This confused Brian. What things? And why was Aunt Phoebe bringing them here? Was she going to live with us?

Then Aunt Phoebe left.

Summer came and Brian went to the pier almost every day. He spent some of his time catching small fish called shiners and sold them to the bait house for a nickel each. He could make enough to buy a sandwich and a drink at the root beer shop down on the beach. Sometimes he would go swimming or meet with some of his school friends.

He would pick shells and sell them to tourists. They would buy almost anything.

There was a passenger boat named The Don that would take tourists out to the Keys. Brian got to know the Captain and if there was room, he would get invited to go out with them. It was not a deep-sea fishing boat although some of the passengers would bring rods and reels then fish off the side, but it was not encouraged. Brian and Captain Dunn would play the "Chart Game". Captain Dunn would look at the chart and say, "There's Cabbage Key" and point in the general direction of the chart.

Brian would look at the chart and ask, "Where?"

Captain Dunn: “Next to Edmont Key.”

Brian would look at again and ask again, “Where?”

“Next to ‘Corn Beef Key’, next to ‘Cabbage Key’,” then he'd laugh because he knew that there was no “Corn Beef Key”.

Brian would laugh because he knew the Captain was kidding.

And then summer was over and Brian had to go back to school. Brian didn't hate school like some of his classmates claimed they did, but he didn't like it much either. He really liked going to the pier and the beach and thought someday he could pilot or captain a boat like The Don.

One day Brian came home from school and Aunt Phoebe was sitting in the living room on mom's chair. She looked older than Brian remembered. She looked tired.

It became clear to Brian that Aunt Phoebe was going to stay, at least for a while. Aunt Phoebe became part of the small family. A few weeks later Aunt Phoebe got a job and would be gone all day and some evenings.

Although Jack didn't like the idea that Aunt Phoebe would be a permanent guest in the house, he came to accept it. Jack and Aunt Phoebe went to work each day so they saw little of each other and all was well for the time being.

It was a few months after Aunt Phoebe moved in when she and Jack had a Saturday off together. Both of their working days were flexible, so it was bound to happen. When Doris knew they would be together for a whole day, she started to make plans. Doris would send Brian off to the movies and then make Jack and Aunt Phoebe sit and talk about their problems. Doris knew that it was all one sided. Jack didn't like Aunt Phoebe and Aunt Phoebe was almost indifferent about it. She knew why

Jack didn't like Aunt Phoebe, but it really didn't matter to Doris except for the tension in the house when Jack and Aunt Phoebe were together.

So one Saturday, Brian was sent to the movies and Doris sat down with Aunt Phoebe and Jack.

“We have to stop ignoring the friction in the family that is being caused by you two,” started Doris.

Jack and Aunt Phoebe looked at each other. Aunt Phoebe said, “I want to tell him.”

“We've been over this before. You promised you would never tell.” replied Jack. There was hurt and anger in Jack's eyes and demeanor. “You can't do this.”

Brian came home from the movies. His mom was sitting on one end of the couch and his dad on the other end. His mom's eyes were red and puffy. Brian could tell she had been crying. His dad's eyes were red. It was obvious he had been crying too, but not as much as his mom’s.

Brian’s mom looked up and said to Brian, “Aunt Phoebe is gone.” She held back a sob. His dad added, “Again.”

“The main reason Santa is so jolly is because he knows where all the bad girls live.”- George Carlin

Dumbing Down of America

I wrote this a few years ago, but it just as relevant today as it was back then.

To identify dates in history I use BCE and CE instead of BC and AD. BCE is "Before the Common Era" and is used instead of BC "Before Christ". CE means "Common Era" and is used instead of AD "Anno Domini," Latin for "in the year of our Lord".

Once again, I hear about the Evangelical view that the earth is only 6000 years old (some say 9000 years old). I assume that this belief is based on the King James version of The Holy Bible. Maybe it is wrong of me to assume, but I've heard it all before from others based on The King James version. Evangelicals are of course, entitled to their belief as are others that also misread and misinterpret The Bible. I admire their belief in their God and in The Bible but they are wrong, wrong about the age of the Earth.

Going through The Bible and adding up the ages of the patriarchs mentioned was a hard job that required a lot of dedication, but it is ignorance of The Bible and its history that those scholars used to come up with the figures that they did.

The Bible is incomplete. There were many books that were not included in the Canon. How many, no one knows for sure. It could have been hundreds and maybe thousands. The choosing of the books to be included was done over a period of one hundred years or so, again it is not known for sure. A note here: The King James version is incomplete. Other versions of The Holy Bible have more books than it does.

It was the Council of Nicaea in 325 CE that put together the Holy Bible. The Council went through all of the books that were reportedly of The Bible. The number of books that were brought to Nicaea is not known, but it is said that all those who attended it brought at least one book. It is generally agreed that the number of attendees was about 1800. Some think that the Council went on to become the Second Council of Nicaea 787 CE. If so, the Council went on for more than 450 years. Later, the

Council of Trent 1545 tackled some of the same issues.

The Bible (any version) is not in chronological order. In the King James version, Genesis 4-22 says Tubal Cain, “an instructor of every artificer, in brass and iron” and in the next chapter 5-3, it says “and Adam lived a hundred and thirty years, and begat a son - - and named him Seth.” The time doesn't jibe. The use of iron didn't start until about 1200 BCE, so that means if the Bible is in chronological order then the Earth is only about 3300 years old. 1200 minus 130 plus 2012. There are written records that are older than 3300 years and written records older than 6000 years also. There are other places in The Bible that show a lack of chronological order.

What does it matter what the Evangelicals teach? They contribute to the dumbing down of America.

“The first thing I do in the morning is brush my teeth and sharpen my tongue.” - Dorothy Parker

www.ingramcontent.com/pod-product-compliance
Ingram Content Group UK Ltd.
Pitfield, Milton Keynes, MK11 3LW, UK
UKHW041839200726
13854UKWH00003BA/1215

9 781716 031861